This book

Matthew

_____

A catalogue record for this book is available from the British Library

Published by Ladybird Books Ltd
80 Strand London WC2R 0RL
A Penguin Company

2 4 6 8 10 9 7 5 3 1
© LADYBIRD BOOKS LTD MMVI
LADYBIRD and the device of a Ladybird are trademarks of Ladybird Books Ltd

ISBN-13: 978-1-84646-087-6
ISBN-10: 1-84646-087-5

Printed in Italy

Puss in Boots

illustrated by Allan Curless

Once upon a time, a father lived with his three sons. When the father died he left each son a special gift.

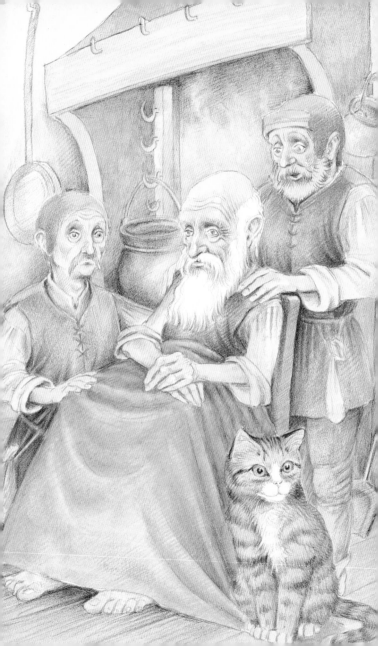

He left his farm to the eldest son. He left his donkey to the middle son. And he left his cat to the youngest son.

The youngest son said, "Puss, my brothers can earn money with their gifts. How can we earn some money?"

9

Puss said, "Master, give me some boots and a bag."

So the boy gave Puss some boots and a bag. Puss put on the boots. Then he went out and caught a rabbit in his bag.

Puss took the rabbit to
the King.

"Here is a gift from my
master," said Puss.

"Who is your master?"
said the King.

"The Marquis of Carrabas
is my master," said Puss.

13

Not long after, Puss went out with the bag again. This time he caught two partridges. Puss took the partridges to the King.

"These two partridges are a gift from my master, the Marquis of Carrabas," said Puss.

"Thank you, Puss in Boots," said the King. "I love to eat partridges."

Soon after, Puss and his master were by a river. Puss saw the King's carriage coming along the road. The King and the Princess were in the carriage.

"Master," said Puss, "take off your clothes and jump into the river."

Then Puss ran to the carriage

"Help me," said Puss. "My master is in the river, and his clothes have been stolen."

21

"We must help the Marquis of Carrabas," said the King. So the King's men helped the boy out of the river.

Then the King said, "We mus take you home." And he put the boy into his carriage.

Puss ran along the road. He saw some men working.

"The King is coming," he said. "You must tell him that the Marquis of Carrabas is your master."

When the King saw the men he said, "Who do you work for?"

"We work for the Marquis of Carrabas," said the men.

When the King had gone, Puss said to the men, "Who lives in that castle?"

The men said, "Our master lives in that castle. He is an ogre."

Puss ran along the road and was soon at the castle. He knocked on the door.

When the ogre came to the door, Puss said, "Can I come in?"

"Come in," said the ogre.
He wanted to eat Puss.

Puss said, "Can ogres
do magic?"

"Just watch!" said the ogre.
And he changed into a lion.

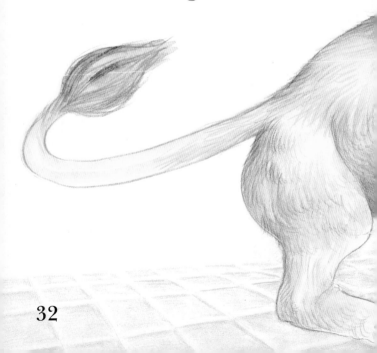

"Is that all the magic you can do?" said Puss. "Change into a mouse."

So the ogre changed into a mouse.

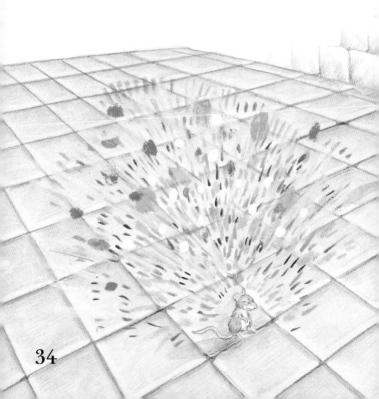

Puss jumped on the mouse
and ate it. Just then, there
was a knock on the door.

When Puss went to the door,
he saw the King, the Princess,
and his master.

"This is my master's castle,"
said Puss.

Not long after, the Princess and the boy fell in love, and were soon married. The boy took the Princess to live at his castle.

So the boy, the Princess, the King and Puss in Boots all lived happily ever after.

43

Read It Yourself is a series of graded readers designed to give young children a confident and successful start to reading.

Level 3 is suitable for children who are developing reading confidence and stamina, and who are ready to progress to longer stories with a wider vocabulary. The stories are told simply and with a richness of language.

About this book

At this stage of reading development, it's rewarding to ask children how they prefer to approach each new story. Some children like to look first at the pictures and discuss them with an adult. Some children prefer the adult to read the story to them before they attempt it for themselves. Many children at this stage will be eager to read the story aloud to an adult at once, and to discuss it afterwards. Unknown words can be worked out by looking at the beginning letter (*what sound does this letter make?*) and the sounds the child recognises within the word. The child can then decide which word would make sense.

Developing readers need lots of praise and encouragement.